1989

VINCE OMNI

1989

Cover design by Emelie Mano.

Interior design by Julianne Johnson.

Red Mare Press / Discover New Art, LLC
70 SW Century Drive, Suite 100442, Bend, Oregon 97702

www.redmarepress.com

Red Mare Press is a division of Discover New Art, LLC.
The Red Mare Press name and logo are trademarks of Discover New Art, LLC. The publisher is not responsible for websites (or their content) that are not owned by the publisher.

ISBN 979-8-9901838-8-9

Printed in the United States of America.

Praise for *1989*

"The magic and power of Vince Omni's pen lies in his masterful conjuring of an era, a place, a people, with specificity and the most intimate of details. Here, Omni takes us back (or introduces us anew) to a moment both different from and similar to our current one, across the fraught terrain of family and community, grappling with longing, regret, forgiveness, and all the complexities of loving, caring for, and failing one another. Omni's characters speak whole worlds of truth in a single line. At turns cool, breathtaking, and heartbreaking, *1989* packs the best kind of emotional punch, unsentimental and unforgettable."

—**Deesha Philyaw**, author of *The Secret Lives of Church Ladies*

"Filled with narrative fast-breaks and winning shots, Omni offers readers a slender but rounded world. Here, through half-spoken memories, the quiet interiority of a nostalgic protagonist clashes and contextualizes major events and shifts in our modern culture. *1989* has something to teach us about the fragility of identity, the scars left by absence, and the strange hope we can find in reclamation."

—**Donald E. Quist**, creator of *Past Ten* and author of *For Other Ghosts*

"I swear the voice in Vince Omni's *1989* leaves the page and begins speaking in your ear. Omni wrote a soul-stirrer with this one."

—**Rion Amilcar Scott**, author of *The World Doesn't Require You*

"The work of Vince Omni delivers the feeling that drives every action, every act of love, and every move on the court. He shows the emotional choreography and improvisation that help the reader see, feel, and inhabit the world on these pages. Time moves as fluidly as the language, taking the story through history, basketball, pop culture, and the urgent immediacy of the times the characters navigate."

—**Ravi Howard**, author of *Like Trees, Walking* and *Driving the King*

"With a searing and controlled voice, our soulful narrator takes us on a powerful and moving journey of grace—grace given and grace denied. This one will leave your heart tender for days. Omni has proven himself a consummate writer. I look forward to seeing him rise."

—**Esther Ifesinachi Okonkwo**, author of *The Tiny Things are Heavier*

For anyone who has ever, rain or shine, hoofed it to a rec center in northeast Denver just to slide into the gym and call out, "Yo, who got next?"

FOREWORD

There is something mesmerizing about watching an impassioned person so deep inside a specific world that all their references and metaphors are refracted through its features and people and customs, their devotion creating a very singular filter. It is why I also halt when my electrician friend halts in a parking garage to point out something magical about the wires overhead, to wax lyrical about circuit breakers and insulators. It is the reverence on their face I am responding to, the same reverence that invites me in. I tell students to write from this kind of specificity—where they find joy, where their characters' obsessions simmer off the page. Now, here is a novelette I can show them, say: See how Vince Omni does it.

The year is 1989. The culture is basketball. The religion is basketball. The language is basketball. Black basketball. See, before this, I didn't know anything about one-handed bounce passes or if a shooting guard was noun or verb, but as a reader, I know how to enjoy tension, I viscerally understand the rush of "nothing but net" after a breathless paragraph of dribbles and midrange shots that spin "around the rim before falling through." I delighted in a heightened state being described like "Isiah Thomas was running a fast break inside my chest…" or a sky described below:

> A riot of purple, pink, and orange filled the darkening sky, like the gods were running a pick-up game and one of them sank a once-in-a-lifetime shot: Dr. J leaping from one side of the court to the other, his arm sweeping the ball beneath the backboard then kissing it off the glass before falling back to earth.

1989 guides us through the world of asymmetrical bobs, cookouts, Hakeem Olajuwon, Cheryl Miller… Our narrator Davyon's revisit to the past is prompted by an interview. A film student making a documentary about his former coach has arrived to ask questions about that time. In the hope of avoiding a more present discomfort, Davyon chooses to return to the sites of memory. For him, though, this significant year wasn't all joy. Back in 1989, there was also escaping bad dads, the isolation of a new place, and homophobia that costs too much. In Davyon's 1989, basketball both saved and forced him outside his comfort zone. The years between then and now have not sanitized memory; time has not answered all questions and I appreciated this resistance to a retrospective all-knowingness when the narrator asks, "What else will I be wrong about?"

With a voice that is smooth, hilarious, and observant, Omni has written a sweet and sad story about mentorship, belonging, and the pain that comes with an expanding understanding of the world. "Or maybe it has something to do with the scarcity of imagination, our failure to grasp the abundance of what could be, that our lives are big enough to hold more than one dream?" This novelette is a kind of coming-of-age story, told from the distance that the bittersweet mellowing of age allows us to access with gentler eyes. All this while Omni continually dunks us in the euphoria of the sport. Yes, the language is basketball but the story is compelling and universal and Omni has succeeded in inviting the rest of the world in. Welcome.

—'Pemi Aguda, Guest Judge

'PEMI AGUDA is from Lagos, Nigeria. She has an MFA from the Helen Zell Writers' Program at the University of Michigan. Her writing has been published in *Granta*, *Zoetrope: All-Story*, *Ploughshares*, and *One Story*, among others, and won O. Henry Prizes. Her novel-in-progress won the 2020 Deborah Rogers Foundation Writers Award. She was a 2021 Fiction Fellow with the Miami Book Fair, a 2022 MacDowell Fellow, and is the current Hortense Spillers Assistant Editor at *Transition Magazine*. Her collection of stories, *Ghostroots* (Norton, 2024), a finalist for the 2024 National Book Award in Fiction, is her first book.

CHURCH CALLED ME A PUSSY six weeks before tryouts. That's what I tell his granddaughter, Raquel, who's sitting across from me in the apartment above my supermarket in northeast Denver on a Saturday morning. She is young, had not even been born when Church called me out my name twenty-six years ago. I don't expect her to know about South Africa, Tiananmen Square, or Reaganomics. It's a Black man in the White House now and a racist with orange hair campaigning to take his place. September 11, social media, and Beyoncé. These are the touchstones of her generation. It's all about context. Hers. Mine. Whatever lies in between. Heat pulses from a lamp hovering above. Two large white umbrellas stand behind Raquel. They catch light, cast it my way, cause sweat to bead up along my neck and forehead. A tall man, Neil, operates a camera beside her. His face is done up like a woman and the reckless length of his earrings calls to mind Bowlegged Lou—minus the Jheri curl and bulging muscles masquerading as self-esteem.

When in doubt, ask about pronouns. Xiomara, my ex-wife, often reminds me of this, on account that there are more than two genders. I'm not sure how that works, but Raquel knows. She signals for Neil to stop recording, sighs, and stares at me through thick-framed glasses that are too big for her serious face. She wrinkles her nose, like someone who's discovered piss in her soy latte.

"Mr. Michaels…"

I ask her to call me Davyon. "Put a mister in front, if it makes you feel better."

"Mr. Michaels, I'm trying to honor the memory of a queer Black man who played twelve seasons in the NBA."

"And I'm just telling you what happened." What I don't say is that she the one tracked me down after Church died in January. Said she came across a video he and I made at the King Center way back when. I was playing ball in that footage, but what Raquel asked of me was different. The thought of answering questions in front of a camera made my ass itch. Cameras always washout my khaki complexion, making me appear lighter than I am. Plus, I'm not much of a talking head. One-on-one, in everyday life? Cool. In front of a camera? Naw. Too public, too impersonal. I almost told Raquel *no.* Then Pops texted he would be in town in a week and wanted to see me. Suddenly, the idea of talking about Church, how he put me on game, felt like the right play. Anything to avoid Pops. I told Raquel I'd do the interview, but we had to do it the second weekend in November. That was a week ago. Now, here she is, all the way up from New Orleans, trying to police how I tell my story. Raquel removes them big-boned glasses, uses the hem of her NYU Film T-shirt to clean the lenses. Could be weighing my words—or getting ready to tell me to kick rocks.

"Okay," she says. "When did all this happen?"

"Friday before Labor Day," I say. "1989." How I know is a month earlier my old man hit Moms for using too much paprika in the potato salad. I went upside his head with a bottle of Seagram's. Pops put a foot in my ass. Moms put me on a bus to Uncle Junior's place here in Denver. Then Church up and called me out my name. Not that he knew my name. Nobody did. I was just some skinny, light-skinned kid in a Kansas City Chiefs T-shirt and a pair of beat-up Nikes. I didn't know his name either. In my head, I called him Jheri Curl. Activator made his hair glow, but it never dripped onto the back of his T-shirt. The one he wore that day was white with black block letters that spelled *Volunteer, MLK Center* on the front and *Parks and Recreation* on the back. He stood on the sideline, beeper clipped to the waistband of his warmups, watching us play like he Doug Moe and we in McNichols Arena and not some rec center in Park Hill. I did my best Fat Lever impersonation and kissed a shot off the glass. Stole an inbound pass next. Ain't had no Alex English to dish it off to, so I drove the lane, steady clocking the basket. Then here come Tyree. Six-five. Solid, too. Like he ate Wheaties. All day, every day. I picked-up my dribble, took my steps, and aimed for the top of the glass. Tyree trapped the ball against the backboard with one hand, dribbled coast-to-coast, cuffed the ball like Dr. J, then rocked the rim. Game over.

"Pussy," Jheri Curl said to me when I walked off the court.

My first instinct was to run up on him. It was one thing to take shit from Pops. It was another thing for this buster to call me out my name. Still, unlike Pops, he had some size on him. Like even if he couldn't squab, he'd have no problem dealing with me.

"Air and opportunity, baby," he said. "Air and opportunity."

"Run it back," I called out, not looking away from him. But brothers were already unlacing kicks, packing up bags, staring at beepers.

Tyree and his homeboys walked my direction. They sported Jackson High practice jerseys, a red ram against a black and gray background. Tyree stopped by the chalkboard to give Jheri Curl some dap.

Jheri Curl looked reserved, like maybe it was someone else he'd rather have standing in front of him. His pager buzzed and he checked it.

Tyree and his boys headed my way next. I held out my hand, ready to say *Nice game*. Woot-di-woot-di-woot.

But the brother shoulder-checked me, knocked me into a wall. His homeboys laughed and taunted me.

Yo, you see them dusty-ass kicks?

Dorothy, you ain't in Kansas no more!

Mark-ass nigga!

I cut across the court to an exit. A weight room stood on the other side of the door. It was small with red walls and black rubber flooring. Jheri Curl's words reverberated in my mind. *Pussy.* I played varsity my freshman year back in Kansas City. If I'd been back home, I'd be competing for a starting spot, not trying to make the team at a new school in a new city. But I ain't had no time for *ifs*, so I bench pressed and imagined myself in a Jackson High jersey, bringing the ball up court, splitting the defense, dropping a no-look pass on my wingman. I busted out squats and pictured myself exploding toward the basket, hands reaching for the rim. I peeped the time and realized I was already half an hour late for work. I imagined Uncle Junior up in my face, breath stinking of cigarettes and Diet Coke.

I was more than an hour late by the time I reached Junior's Grocery Store in the Dahlia Square. Someone had tagged CMG Blood on the wall next to the door. Inside, Junior stood bent over a box, wheezing. Sweat sprouted along the edge of his receding hairline. More boxes stood on either side of him. They clogged the aisle. A cart full of broken-down boxes sat near the meat counter. Junior stood with a grunt. He had this way of looking through me, like he saw me but wasn't really seeing me. At least, that's how it felt back then. It ain't occur to me until later, that this was a holdover from his days as an all-city point guard for Jackson High—a million Twinkies ago.

"It ain't my fault," I said.

"I'm docking your check," Junior said.

"Check?" I'd been working for three weeks and had yet to see a dime.

"Excuse me?" a customer called from the register.

Junior nodded and I flattened myself against the shelves, knocking over cans of Spaghetti-Os, so I could slide by him and get to the register. A girl my age stood on the other side of the counter. She wore a hairstyle that swept down the back of her neck and erupted into a riot of stiff curls up top. It made her look like MC Lyte, only darker. She smiled when I greeted her. White teeth. Smooth, brown skin. I tried not to stare while I rang up her items—five pounds of ground beef, four packs of hot links, three slabs of ribs, a few loaves of white bread, several bags of chips, and ten packs of Kool-Aid. The kind of things Moms would buy for Labor Day. I thought about Pops firing up the grill, Frankie Beverly and Maze flowing from speakers, a glass of gin in one hand, a pair of tongs in the other.

"That's my mama's favorite song."

I looked up from bagging her groceries. "Say what, now?"

"'Before I Let Go,'" she said. "You were just humming it."

Heat flashed across my face.

"You're cute when you blush," she said. It was something Moms would have said and that made me smile.

"And dimples, too!"

I ain't know what to say to that, so I took the cash she held out to me, made change, and handed it to her with a receipt. Junior kept a cup of pens on the counter for customers to write checks. The girl plucked one up, wrote something on the back of the receipt, and handed it to me.

"You should come by my house for Labor Day," she said with a wink.

I watched her walk away.

Junior slapped the back of my neck. "Quit eye-hoeing my customers, boy."

The back of the receipt read *Gigi.* Her phone number and address were there too.

It was nearly ten o'clock when we climbed the stairs to Junior's apartment above the store, our arms filled with canned pasta, lunchmeat, and a loaf of bread. We ate on the sofa in front of the television, watching a VHS of the 1987 Eastern Conference Finals, Game 5. It was the fourth time we'd seen it since I moved in. Junior liked the physical play between the Pistons and Celtics. Each time we watched it, it felt like he was seeing it for the first time. He even acted surprised when Larry Bird picked off Isiah Thomas's inbound pass and dished it off to Dennis Johnson for the winning bucket.

"Your mama called today." It was halftime and Junior stood in the kitchen, layering more lunchmeat and cheese between slices of bread.

I sat on the sofa, watching a replay of Robert Parish going upside Bill Laimbeer's head for a cheap shot to the throat.

"They want you to come home."

It shook me how Parish and Laimbeer could go after each other like that and not pick up fouls.

"You hear what I said, boy?"

I paused the tape. "What about hoop?" It was what we discussed most back then, safer than processing my being there in his tiny apartment above a supermarket.

Junior made a show of putting his sandwich together, wiping his hands, and blowing out a long stream of air. "Too much competition here. You got a better chance back in KC, where the coach knows you."

He was right, but what he didn't understand, or maybe what I hadn't known myself, was that I would make the team at home, but I couldn't make Pops give up gin. *I can't breathe.* That's what Santana, my older brother, said when he joined the marines that spring. My younger sisters, Aisha and Alisha, were in no hurry to leave. Pops loved the twins, never even raised his voice to them. But me? *Why should I go back to that house?* I could have asked Junior that question. Instead, I looked across the living room where his Jackson High jersey hung in a frame.

"Just let me try out," I said. "If I don't make it, I'll go back next semester."

He stood akimbo, which was what Moms would do when studying on her next move.

"Fine," he said with a sigh. "I'll talk to your mama. But you work for me Mondays, Wednesdays, Fridays, and Saturdays."

I'd already worked one Saturday. Old folks from the Zion Senior Center filled the store with the creak of walkers and the scent of BENGAY. A few of them stood in front of the meat counter sorting through food stamps and haggling over the price of cold cuts. I thought the day would never end.

"Every Saturday?" I asked.

"You do for me, I do for you."

We shook hands, then he spooned the rest of the ravioli into his bowl.

"Yo, I was gonna get seconds."

"Told you I was gonna tax that check."

I washed dishes, unfolded the sofa, then turned on the TV. I thought about calling Gigi, but it was after midnight. Plus, I ain't know what to say to her. Hours earlier, she'd smiled at me for the first time. Now there I was wondering when I'd see that light again. I distracted myself with *The Arsenio Hall Show*. It was a rerun: Mr. Miyagi from *The Karate Kid*, and MC Hammer with Oaktown 357. I fell asleep before Hammer performed. In my dreams, I was Daniel-san, only with light-brown skin, a high-top fade, and a rat tail. I wore a gi with a headband and sneakers. A referee handed me a ball on the sideline then blew his whistle. Bill Laimbeer called for the rock in front of the basket. I zipped it over Danny Ainge's head. Then Jheri Curl swooped in for the steal. That old Ready-for-the-World-looking nigga was starting to get on my nerves.

"Wait," Raquel says now. "Ready for the World?"

"R&B group," I say.

"Right! They sang that song about Sheila!" Neil says from behind the camera, his frohawked head nodding up and down. "My mother has the vinyl. Bunch of wet and wavy dudes in bad suits."

A notification flashes across the screen of my phone. I open my messages and find a blue dot next to the name David Jasper. *Hey, son. I know you're busy this weekend, but I decided to come anyway. Hoping you got a minute to chop it up with your old man. Let me know.*

"Davyon?" Neil asks, pulling me away from my phone.

"My bad," I say, laying the phone on my coffee table. "What's up?"

"Ready for the World?" Neil arches an eyebrow.

"Right. Lead singer spoke like James Bond, so I think they were from the UK."

"Says here they're from Flint." Raquel holds her phone out for me to see.

I hunch forward, read that the band is, in fact, from Flint, Michigan. Blood rushes to my face. This story is only going to get more complicated. If I am wrong about something as simple as Ready for the World, what else will I be wrong about?

"Listen to the song," I say, leaning back in my chair. "You'll see what I mean."

"I will," Raquel says. "But, right now, we're talking about Labor Day weekend, 1989."

I spent most of Saturday behind the meat counter, ducking in and out of the cooler, working the slicer or grinder, wrapping up cold cuts and ground beef in white butcher paper. I peeped an old man count then recount a handful of food stamps. He ordered a pound of hogshead cheese. I sliced up a pound and a quarter. He insisted that I price it all at one pound even. I rolled my eyes.

"Not my fault you back there slicing all willy-nilly," the old man said.

"How about we give it to you half off, Mr. Hyde," Junior said. He sidled up next to me, cheesing like he the mayor. The old man thanked him, and I started off down the platform to see about another customer.

"I got it," Junior said, then handed me a piece of paper. "Fill and deliver this order ASAP." I read the customer's name. *Elijah Church*. Sounded familiar, like someone I should know. Junior left instructions at the bottom of the page. *Call before you leave the store!* I packed-up the groceries: grits, instant coffee, Corn Flakes, bananas, orange juice, bread, eggs, and a pound of bacon. Then I loaded up Junior's truck and drove off without calling.

Elijah Church lived in the back half of a goldbrick duplex on Holly Street, just north of Martin Luther King Jr. Boulevard. The lawn was small but neat. A smooth unbroken sidewalk led to the front porch. The door was open. Inside, two dudes kissed in the living room. I ain't talking about Magic and Isiah smooching cheeks at half court. One of these dudes had a hand down the other's pants. I knocked. One cat jumped up and ran to the back of the house. The other, Jheri Curl, pulled a pack of Kool's from his pocket and lit one.

"Elijah Church?" I asked.

He nodded, motioned for me to come inside.

I sat the bags on the porch, walked back to the truck, and drove away. Didn't even think to get the money he owed for groceries.

Junior said Church had a prepaid account. *I probably owe him money.*

I fixed my mouth to say something about what I'd seen but changed my mind. That was Church's business.

I just couldn't believe he'd called me a pussy when his punk ass was the one busting slob with another dude.

"So," Raquel says now. "Are you still homophobic?"

Why I look to Neil for help, I don't know. Neither does he. He shrugs and says, "Still rolling."

"That was twenty-six years ago," I say. "I was just sixteen, had never even heard of that word."

"So that justifies your attitude?" Raquel asks.

I shake my head. "Ignorance is not innocence."

"It's sin," Raquel says. She cocks her head toward my bookshelves. The apartment is nicer than when Junior was alive. I updated the kitchen and bathroom, switched out the carpet for hardwoods, and installed a library where Junior kept his VHS collection. A few tapes remain on the built-in shelves. Raquel ignores them, running her fingers instead along a row of books. "Any Robert Browning in this collection?"

"Is that who said that?" I ask. "Thought it was Tupac."

Neil suppresses a laugh.

"Okay," Raquel says, scanning her notes. "What happened with Gigi?"

Gigi lived in the nice part of Park Hill. Grass shined inside manicured borders and late-model cars sat in wide, clean driveways. A grip of them were parked outside the address written on the receipt in my hand. The house was white with wide red-brick steps leading up to a large porch with columns that formed archways across the front of the house. Music drifted out to the street.

I ain't much on Casanova

Me and Romeo ain't never been friends

It was dancing in the backyard. Men and women snapping fingers, shifting this way and that, or two-stepping to the beat. Not like how they do in Kansas City, with men leading women in twists and turns and intricate foot patterns that would have given Hakeem Olajuwon the blues. I never could step, but Pops was cold with it. I used to watch him spin Moms on our patio during cookouts just like this one. Each step for them was like a needle in the groove of a record, each move like what music would look like if it was six-two with brown skin, a crooked smile, and a do-rag line creased across its forehead, or petite with light skin, thick red hair, and eyes that flashed with every dip and turn. Pops tried to teach me once, but I didn't want to learn from him, didn't like the way he looked away from Moms when they stepped, like having her there with him, their bodies in sync, wasn't magic.

Gigi's mother walked up to me, shook my hand, then said, "I'm Dr. Hawkins." Said she was the assistant principal at Jackson High then spun around before I could tell her I would start at her school the next day. I followed her past the grill where a guy in a T-shirt and Bermuda shorts stood drinking beer. A tattoo of the Marine Corps logo occupied one of his biceps. He pointed two fingers at his eyes, then pointed those fingers at me. Dr. Hawkins slapped his arm playfully.

"This is my friend Mike," she said. "Ignore him."

Inside, trays of food covered in foil paper littered every surface of the kitchen. I fixed myself a plate and went downstairs, which was a finished basement complete with sofa, television, stereo, a pool table, and at least a dozen people. Gigi greeted me with a hug then led me over to a chair. She wore a brown and gold Thomas Jefferson High School t-shirt and a pair of gold boxers over spandex shorts, which was the style back then. Her hair was now styled in an asymmetric bob that covered one eye.

Donnie Simpson was on TV. I sat down and ate. The ribs and chicken were dry, but the hot links were good, and the beans were spicy and sweet. I went back for seconds, washing everything down with a Coke and trying to keep up with Gigi and her friends. They sat on surfaces Pops would never allow—coffee table, end tables, arms of the sofa—and talked about movies, music, a cross-eyed math teacher who saw them even when he did not look at them. One girl wore a T-shirt that read *Free South Africa*. She eyed the soda in my hand and asked if I supported apartheid.

"Excuse me?"

"Coca-Cola, brother," she said. "Mandela will never be free until Coke divests."

"Girl, stop!" Gigi forced a laugh. "This is a party, not a rally."

I went to the pool table, where most of the brothers stood. One of them handed me a cue stick, but I waved it off.

"Can't play pool," I said.

"Can't hoop, either." The voice came from behind me. I turned to find Tyree and his entourage coming down the stairs. He appeared larger than he'd been a few days earlier, when he pushed me into a wall. I couldn't take him in a fight, but I didn't care about winning. I only cared how it felt like Isiah Thomas was running a fast break inside my chest, how blood pounded in my ears, how my fingers curled into fists.

Gigi was suddenly at my side, her hand on one of my forearms. "Quit starting trouble, Ty." There was a tease in her voice, like she was happy to see him.

"Wayz out, nigga," Tyree said, extending his hand toward me for some dap. "Just fucking with you, Dorothy."

Gigi, car keys in hand, led me upstairs, out the back door, and around the front of the house to a Honda Civic. She apologized for Tyree while she drove. *We've known each other since third grade. Our parents thought we would get married one day. We dated for a minute last year. It didn't work out, but we're still friends.* She pulled into an empty parking lot on a hill overlooking the city, guiding the Civic into a lonely spot behind a religious building and killed the engine. We sat in silence for a few minutes, waiting for the sun to put on a show. I drew a long, deep breath then released it. Tension slowly slipped away from my body. Gigi must have felt it because she leaned over and kissed me. I kissed her back, soft at first, but then for real, with feeling. I didn't want to stop, but when she reached for my zipper, I told her to do just that.

"What's wrong?" she asked, a little breathless.

"Ain't we at a church?"

"Synagogue," she said. "Are you Jewish?"

What I was was scared. What I said was, "Maybe we should slow down."

"Relax," she said, leaning my seat back.

Outside, the sun splashed down in the west, casting the city into the shadow of the Rockies. A riot of purple, pink, and orange filled the darkening sky, like the gods were running a pick-up game and one of them sank a once-in-a-lifetime shot: Dr. J leaping from one side of the court to the other, his arm sweeping the ball beneath the backboard then kissing it off the glass before falling back to earth.

Raquel leans forward now. She clicks her pen open and shut several times. "Why were you so nervous about being alone with Gigi?"

I curse myself for becoming caught up, for revealing this detail to her. Now a woman young enough to be my daughter—if I'd been a teen father—is asking me intimate questions in my home.

"Were you really attracted to her?"

"What do you think?" I want her to say it.

"Well, you did have that dream about my grandfather."

"Not that kind of dream." I don't tell her that when I was nine, I thought I was gay because I loved Pops and I could not reconcile that love with the lust I felt when paging through a stash of *Playboy* magazines I found in the garage.

"The subconscious is very powerful," Neil says.

"I thought y'all came here to learn more about Church?"

"We did," Raquel says. "But your story is part of his story."

"A small part." At least, that's how it felt until I began to unpack it. Now, I strain under a weight I hadn't fully considered.

"We can circle back to you and Gigi later." Raquel jots something down in her notebook. "How was your new school. Jackson High, right?"

It was a big fight the first day. Dr. Hawkins squawked out commands through a bullhorn. *Move along! Calm Down! Stop!* By then, it was homies with blue flags squaring up with homies flying red ones. It was a grip of them, on both sides, brothers and sisters loc'd out with creased khakis and Nike Cortez sneakers. The police came. So did the families. Someone's brother, uncle, cousin rolled into the parking lot in a Buick Regal and skidded to a stop in a no-parking zone. I was straight bugging. It felt like a Wild West flick.

I went to each class and, even though I could leave campus for lunch, I ate in the cafeteria: a gray hamburger patty in a dry bun, chips, chocolate milk, and cookies packed in a wax-paper sleeve. I sat across from a table of basketball players in the corner of the cafeteria. Coach Mountainside stood like a tree next to them. He was a Black man with skin tinged red and thick arms folded over a broad chest, dispensing bits of wisdom. *Keep them grades up. Always use a rubber. Anybody asks, them sneakers came from a booster club, not a booster.* He winked here and his face, which came with a nose like the one I used to find on the cover of my Big Chief notebook, cracked into a wide smile.

The King Center was dead after school, but I didn't care. I had just gone three-and-a-half days without the smell of rubber, the squeak of sneakers, or the rhythm of hands slapping the glass. The court was nearly empty. Some tall, lanky chick with a with an afro, looking like a bootleg Cheryl Miller, threw up bricks like she was building projects. I told her so.

She palmed the ball, backed up to the free throw line, took her steps, then dunked with one hand.

"Shoot for it," I said, itching to play.

She bricked again.

I put down some ground rules: one point per shot, two if it's from behind the arc; make-it-take-it; first to fifteen wins.

I hit a couple of buckets near the free-throw line, made Bootleg Cheryl leave the paint to play defense. Her feet thudded against the court, and she straightened her back when she approached. I slipped past homegirl for an easy bucket. I was up five points before she blocked one of my shots, backed me down into the paint and scored. We traded buckets until I was up, fourteen to ten. I checked the ball, hit her with a crossover, then sped to the hoop. One step, two step, left-foot jump, right-hand finger roll.

"Game!" I turned toward the sidelines to see if anyone else had come in only to find Church standing there. He ain't say nothing, but his insult from a few days earlier still bounced around inside my head.

"Run it back," Bootleg Cheryl said. We played again. I smoked her fifteen to five. Then I ran through three brothers who'd just come in. One of them had on a Jackson High practice jersey.

Church ain't said a word.

Later, I shot free throws while he swept the floor. Whatever magic I'd been working earlier was gone.

Each time I hit a shot the next one clanged off the rim and bounced over by the door. Church stopped sweeping and posted up beneath the basket.

"Put your elbow in and spread your fingers." He said it just like that, like he ain't stand over there a few days earlier and dog me out to my face.

"Ain't nothing sweet over here, old man," I said.

"I'm trying to help, young blood. If you just—"

I walked off, dribbling the ball hard all the way down to the other end of the court.

The next day was Wednesday. Five days since Church called me out my name. I was straightening the cereal aisle, thinking about the next time I would see Gigi, when Junior handed me another list with Church's name on it.

"Nah," I said. "I don't fuck with that nigga."

Junior popped me upside my head. "Who is you talking to?"

Tears welled up in my eyes. I squared up with him, balled my hands into fists.

"I wish you would," he said then stuffed the list into my apron pocket.

I filled the order, shoving items into bags, then drove over to Holly Street. I pounded on the door then set the bags down on the porch and turned toward the sidewalk. A screen door whined behind me.

"Young blood," Church called to me.

I kept walking.

"Don't have me call Junior."

I stopped, turned around.

He stepped out onto the porch in a mesh tank top. The muscles in his arms, shoulders, and chest glided beneath his brown skin. He pulled a ten-dollar bill from his pocket, held it out to me, then gestured to the bags huddled down by the door. "Those go next door to Ms. Rita." He nodded to the duplex in front of his.

I mugged him for minute.

He mugged me back, that air-and-opportunity look.

A cigarette hung from the corner of Ms. Rita's mouth when she answered her door. She wore a house dress and a burgundy wig that clashed with dry, golden skin. A pair of reading glasses threatened to fall off the tip of her nose and, when I looked at her good, it seemed that her head shook without her knowing. I helped her put away groceries and make instant coffee. She offered me a five-dollar bill, which I folded into the ten I'd just taken from Church.

That night, a found a stack of VHS tapes on the kitchen counter next to half a frozen pizza. The tapes were bound together by a rubber band. A note from Junior was stuck to one side. *After you finish your homework.* I read each tape's label: *Elijah Church, Jackson High, 1968*; *Elijah Church, University of Oregon*; and *Elijah Church, NBA*. It was this last tape that triggered my memory. Me and

Santana on the floor in front of the TV. Pops wouldn't let us on furniture back then, said we didn't know how to sit on it right. He sat behind us in his chair. On screen, Elijah Church, who played for Cleveland back then, gave Kansas City the business. He scored more points than Eddie Johnson, grabbed more boards than LaSalle Thompson, and dropped more dimes than Larry Drew. Pops turned off the game midway through the third quarter and told us to go to bed.

I set the tapes aside and ate with my books open on the counter. There was a geometry quiz to study for, a list of vocabulary words from biology to memorize, and a chapter from *The Clan of the Cave Bear* to read.

I went to bed around midnight. Outside, voices rose from the projects across the street. Bass from a passing car thudded against the night. I felt its vibration in bed. I imagined sound waves shooting out the back of somebody's trunk, rearranging molecules and atoms, rippling across the atmosphere like a tsunami. I closed my eyes and was back in Kansas City standing over Pops, the jagged edge of that Seagram's bottle still in my hand. He laughed then sprung to his feet. His fist exploded against my eye. Then there was the scrape of chairs against linoleum. A jumble of voices and footfall behind me. I fought to free myself from a tangle of arms. Later, Moms, her face wet, drove me to the Greyhound station. She didn't even get out of the car.

I got up and popped the first tape into the VCR. Church, tall and thin with close-cut hair, dominated the Jackson High championship game, pulling up from deep, driving to the basket, dishing to the open man. One pass, a one-handed bounce pass, he laced through a defender's legs on a fast break. He finished the game with thirty-one points, ten assists, and twelve boards. The Oregon Ducks tape was also legit. His body had thickened up a little, filling out his uniform. Instead of running point, he played shooting guard or small forward. He'd improved his stroke, too, making the net sing with shots from fifteen feet or deeper. The NBA tape featured his debut for Seattle. They played Utah. He worked through first-quarter jitters, throwing the rock out of bounds, and shooting an airball. He hit a couple buckets in the second quarter, dropped five dimes, too, before exploding for ten points and three assists in the third quarter. He finished the game with nineteen points, nine assists, and eight boards. I clicked off the television and went back to bed. My eyes grew heavy, but an idea floated on the edge of my consciousness.

Thursday. Church sat on a stool behind the front desk when I walked into the King Center after school. He bent over the counter and read a newspaper. I showed him my ID card.

"Umm hmm," he said, steady reading.

"Look, you know, I just want to apologize for how I acted the other day."

He licked his thumb, turned the page of his paper.

"I'ma tryout at Jackson High this year and I was wondering if—"

"I look like Mr. Miyagi to you?" Church asked.

"Say what?"

"Do I look like a short, bald Japanese man?"

"No. I was just hoping—"

His beeper went off. He checked it then shut himself in an office behind the counter.

Friday. Five weeks until tryouts. I stood at that free-throw line, tried to recall the advice Church had given me about my elbow and my fingers. Then here come Tyree and them. I setup for a free throw then pulled the trigger.

"Brick," one of Tyree's homeboys called out.

"Nah, nigga," another one said. "That shit was a yellow brick."

They fell out laughing.

Church entered the gym, newspaper tucked under his arm.

Tyree called out his name, nodded.

I clocked Church's response, the slow nod, the stiff smile. He didn't really like Tyree. We had that much in common. I walked up to Tyree, passed him the ball. "Shoot for it."

"Your game's too young for that conversation," he said.

"I'll shoot for it," I said. "If I make it, we play."

He smirked, looked at his boys like, *this nigga*, but agreed when he saw I was serious.

I dribbled over to the top of the key, tucked my elbow in, lined it up with the basket, spread my fingers, and let it fly. Nothing but net.

Tyree crossed me up on the first play then dunked the ball. I checked the ball up top, hit him with that dribble hesitation then slipped by him to my right. He picked my pocket, turned around and nailed a midrange shot. I checked the ball again, crossed him up, and went left, then pulled up for a shot that spun around the rim before falling through the net. I managed a few more buckets, but it wasn't enough. Same time it took me to hustle-up five points, he dropped fifteen without breaking a sweat.

"Talk to me when your game grow up," Tyree said. "Fucking faggot."

Church waited for me at the free-throw line when I walked back to the other end of the court. He called for the ball, motioned for me to stand next to him. I hesitated. Yeah, I asked for his help, but I hadn't considered that for him to help me I'd have to stand next to him.

"I can't Miyagi you from over there, young blood," Church said.

I walked over to the free-throw line. He stood behind me and I moved up a little bit.

"Gotta stay behind the line."

I stepped back, assumed a shooting stance. He circled me. I tensed up. He nudged my elbow. I flinched.

"Relax, young blood." He leaned in a bit, lowered his voice. "You ain't really my type."

I cracked a smile.

"We good?"

I nodded.

Church passed me the ball then stood behind me. He gripped my wrist with one hand, held it firm, and that firmness steadied me, calmed my nerves. He showed me how to spread my fingers along the ball's pebbled surface, how to line up my elbow and lace-up a shot, and how to release the ball off the tips of my fingers. I then stood halfway between the free-throw and the bucket, left arm behind my back, shooting one-handed while he critiqued my form.

Bend your knees!

Snap that wrist!

Nigga, is you shooting the ball, or is you throwing it?

I shot a hundred baskets before he let me go back to the free-throw line.

Down court, Tyree executed a tomahawk dunk.

"Sure you wanna do this?" Church asked.

I turned back toward my basket and sunk one free throw. Then another. Then another.

⁓⁓⁓

WE STOP FILMING LATE SATURDAY afternoon. Raquel and Neil want to hit up the Diaspora Café in Five Points. It used to be a diner that served the best chili in the city. Now it's a bougie coffee shop with black-bean burgers, lamb kebabs, and sweet potato scones. Raquel invites me to join them for a working dinner. I beg off, promising to share everything I know tomorrow.

"We're rewatching footage Sunday," Raquel says. "But we're cleared with Parks and Rec to film at the King Center on Monday. Nine o'clock work for you?"

"See you then," I say.

Downstairs, I check in with Xiomara. My ex-wife is half Black, half Mexican, and all business, which is why we still have a professional relationship ten years after our divorce. We were still married when I inherited the store after Junior died. First thing I did was hire Xiomara. She'd helped turn her family's taqueria into a chain of shops across the metro, so I knew she could handle marketing, recruitment, training, and public relations. Today, we discuss inventory, payroll, the training schedule for new cashiers, and Thanksgiving end caps. A grip of shoppers floods the store around six o'clock, but I don't mind. Just knowing Pops is in town conjures up the stink of gin and the press of his anger. My shoulders tense up, the hair on the back of my neck prickles, and I must remind myself to breathe. So, I bag groceries, corral carts, open another register when lines grow long, and customers cast their eyes about the store for relief.

"You okay, D?" Xiomara asks before I climb the stairs to my apartment at the end of the night, a to-go container filled with mac n'cheese in one hand. "How's David?"

"Excuse me?"

"Mama Yvonne told me he'd be here this weekend."

I usually like the fact that Xiomara still speaks with Moms.

"Ain't got nothing to say to that man," I say.

"Fine. Talk to someone else."

One of Xiomara's missions in life is to get me into therapy. I don't have the heart to tell her I've tried twice already. Once with a white woman who approached our sessions like an anthropological study of Blackness, and a second time with an Asian man who wanted to prescribe me meds within five minutes of my sitting down in his office.

"Not now, Xi," I say.

She kisses my cheek. I resist the urge to pull her close. Rule one: She makes the first move. Rule two: No bumping uglies at the store—not even my apartment.

Hotels are best. I like the venues with complimentary breakfast. Waffle irons remind me of a childhood when Saturday morning meant cartoons and a big breakfast. Last week, we checked into an artsy economy number near downtown. One weekend, we splurged on the Four Seasons, ordering room service when one hunger, finally sated, gave way to another. We talk about everything but our old life and her new one. We are better lovers now that she has a husband and two kids.

Upstairs, I listen to a voicemail from Pops. I wait for the timbre of his gruff baritone, but it's a woman's voice I hear in the background. *What can I get you, hon?* This question calls to mind dark rooms with long bars and shelves of amber liquors backlit by soft light. A muffling sound then, finally, Pops is there. "Hey, son. Just trying to catch up with you. I'm at the Double Tree by the old airport. Man, things sure have changed since the last time I been here." That was 1993, when he'd taken Aisha and Alisha back-to-school shopping. He was like that with them—doting. Gave them anything they wanted. Even paid their way through school. Today, Aisha is a pediatrician, and Alisha is an exec at Kansas City Power and Light, the same company Pops retired from as a lineman. His devotion to my sisters has not absolved him of his foulness. Aisha, knife in hand, once stood between him and our mother. Alisha, his favorite, sicced the law on him twice. "Anyway," his recorded voice says. "I'll be here 'til Tuesday morning. Hope I can see you before I hit the road."

I text Pops. *Long day today. Maybe tomorrow.*

He texts back. *We can break bread. Is that diner in Five Points still open?*

I send him a link to the Diaspora Café. *It's a coffee shop now.*

I call up his profile on social media, where I find his brown face smiling under a baseball cap that reads John 3:16. The other details, I already know. *Hometown: Kansas City, MO. Studied at: U.S. Marines. Hoorah! Occupation: Deacon, Holy Redeemer Church of God in Christ. Spouse: Yvonne Jasper.* I click on my mother's profile. Her face, light and dotted with liver spots, populates on my screen. Her's is the smile of the long suffering. Tentative, as if things might fall apart before she's had a chance to refresh her feed. I call her.

"You speak with your father yet?" This she asks by way of hello.

"Why are you telling Xiomara my business?"

"Why are you avoiding my question?"

"Do you know what he wants?"

She sighs. "All I know is he visited Santana in Virginia last week and now your brother, his husband, and their children are coming to Thanksgiving."

When Pops stopped drinking five years ago, he found Jesus. He also joined Keepers of the Promise, a Christian men's group that condemns homosexuality. He banned Santana from the house so long as he *practiced that sinful lifestyle*. I haven't been home since.

"That's good for Santana," I say. "But I got nothing to say to David Jasper."

Moms chides me for calling Pops by his government name. "Maybe he'll be the one talking."

"He can't say nothing I want to hear."

"No, but he might say something you need to hear."

I can think of no reply to that observation, so Moms explains that she and my sisters are meeting for brunch tomorrow to plan Thanksgiving. "If you show this year, the whole family will be there. I'm making Hopping John, Aisha will do the yams, and you know Alisha can't even make a bowl of Corn Flakes, so she'll probably bring a dessert from one of them fancy places she likes."

The silence that follows holds enough disappointment to span the 600 miles of highway stretched out between us.

"He's trying, D. He sees a therapist twice a month at the VA," Moms says. She reminds me that it's been five years since he's had a drink. Five years since last he put his hands on her and she went upside his head with a rolling pin. "If I can forgive him, the least you can do is hear him out."

I want to ask her if Pops ever asked for her forgiveness, or if he just worked that out with Jesus. I tell her instead that I am tired, then promise to think about Thanksgiving. I call Santana next. When he doesn't pick up, I text him.

David is here, blowing up my phone. Call me ASAP.

The thought of driving my fist through drywall, of feeling its chalky firmness giving way to the force of my knuckles, occurs to me. The last time I'd felt this way was eight years ago, when Xiomara told me she was remarrying. I had never expected us to get back together, but I had also never expected how hard regret would hit me. I congratulated her that night. Swallowed my regret with a smile, waited for her to leave, then walked upstairs and punched holes in my living room wall until its surface stood pocked with pits and craters and tiny cuts blossomed along the ridges of my fists. Tonight, I grab a gym bag, head out to my car, and drive to a 24-hour gym, where I go a few rounds with the heavy bag.

I sleep in late Sunday, then go for a run. Later, when I have showered, I watch television until I fall asleep. It is dark when I awake. Messages from Pops choke my text feed. I turn off the phone without reading them, then go downstairs in a tank-top and boxers to raid the deli. I have already plated two pieces of fried chicken and potato salad when I hear a truck idling outside. Back in the day, the Dahlia boasted a skating rink, a Louisiana kitchen, and an urban mens store ran by Koreans. Today, it holds senior housing, a health center, and mental health offices.

Traffic is moderate during the week, but slow on the weekend—especially Sunday nights.

At a bank of monitors in the security office, I adjust the zoom of the parking lot camera until I see a Harley-Davidson pickup with big wheels. Pops bought a used one just like it back in 2009, when an ice storm left a swathe of Kansas City without power. He keeps it in tip-top condition. Even has a vanity plate. I can just make it out when I adjust the zoom: LINEMAN. I eat and monitor Pops, which is when Santana texts me back.

Yeah, he was here too.

And now you're going home for Thanksgiving?

We sat down. We talked. It was good.

You a better man then me.

I'm a father with two kids who want to know their grandparents.

What did he say?

Too much for me to text. Talk to him.

You sound like Moms.

Early morning. TTYL.

On the monitor, Pops tosses something out the window. I zoom in and find several crushed cans on the ground. I can't make out the logo, but I don't have to.

Sober my ass.

—————

THE KING CENTER IS DIFFERENT nowadays. The front desk has been moved, but the weight room is in the same place, as is the gym, though I am shocked to find it filled with pickleball players. Raquel, dressed in gym clothes, speaks with a worker on the sidelines, phone held out so that the man can read her screen. Fifteen minutes later, all pickleball players and their nets are gone. I shoot buckets at one end of the court while Raquel and Neil set up at the other end. It doesn't take long to find my rhythm. One bucket turns into five, turns into fifteen, turns into thirty. It's like Church is here with me, rebounding the ball, telling me to breathe, to square my body to the basket, follow-through on my release. When I look up, I see Neil on the sideline, camera trained on me.

"Haven't lost your shot," Raquel says, walking onto the court.

I want to tell her exactly what I've lost. Instead, I pass her the ball. She calls glass, banks in a left-handed twelve-footer, holding her release for good measure.

"Church taught you that?"

She nods. "Let's talk about what he taught you."

I didn't shoot much that first week of training. I jumped rope, five hundred skips each day. I ran suicides, baseline to baseline, slapping each line in between with both palms. I performed a grip of calisthenics and plyometrics. The only time I touched the rock was when I played one-on-one with Church, and even then, I played defense on every play.

Watch my stomach, not the ball!

You reach, you get beat!

Slide your feet, goddammit!

It was *plant your foot* the following week, when we drilled layups from every angle: right side, left side, down the middle, reverse layups from both directions. I was getting up there next to the rim, too, slapping the glass, which meant that Church would let me play offense during one on one, routinely kicking my ass by ten points.

I'll never know why Gigi showed up one day. If she knew Church, she would have known better than to sashay up and down the sideline, cheering my name. She would not have been surprised when he told her to leave, would not have looked from him to me in disbelief.

"Pussy is a distraction," Church said when she left the gym.

The gym was suddenly too quiet. I dribbled the ball.

"Oh," Church said. "You ain't had none yet."

Looking back, I can see how obvious it must have been. I was gangly, awkward, hella-shy. What else could I have been but a virgin? Gigi wanted to help me out in that department, but I was scared. What if I wasn't big enough? What if she didn't like the way I did it? What if she gave me a disease? What if I got her pregnant? What if we had a baby and I turned into Pops, a man who could no longer see magic, even when it lived in his house, ate his food, slept next to him in bed?

Church swiped the ball away mid-bounce. I assumed a defensive stance. He backed me down into the paint, hit me with a double pump, but I stripped the ball, dribbled to the top of the key, and nailed a jumper.

"Not bad," he said, the promise of a smile on his face. "Listen, ain't nothing wrong with being inexperienced." He checked the ball and assumed a defensive stance. "But this ass whooping you 'bout to get fitna to be downright criminal."

We watched tape at Church's place, footage from his days in the league. He showed me how to stop and rewind plays, to question details I might have missed the first time. Why was Nate Archibald wide open at the top of the key? Why didn't the defense follow Bill Laimbeer when he cut across the baseline? How does Walter Davis create enough space to hit that jumper off the wing? His crib was small but neat: matching couch and chair, glass coffee table and end tables, and an entertainment center that held a television and stereo system. A picture of a brown-skinned girl in a school blazer stood on top of the television. She wore her hair in French braids and her smile revealed crooked teeth in braces.

"Niece?" I asked one afternoon.

"Celeste," he said. "My babygirl."

I must have looked confused.

"Never said I didn't like women." He said Celeste lived with her mother, his ex-wife, down in Louisiana.

Church opened what looked like an old family bible, the kind with a picture of white Jesus on the cover and the names of the Black people it belonged to written on the dedication page. Only this bible was hollow in the middle, where a wooden box sat. Church opened the box and retrieved a small baggie. He dumped its contents on the coffee table, releasing a musky odor that made me think of the homies passing around a blunt in the school bathroom.

"That why your beeper keep going off?"

"Nope." He handed me the pager. "It's for Celeste."

I read the screen. "Fourteen?"

"Flip it."

I did, then saw that an upside-down 14 spells *hi* on a pager. "Y'all must be close?"

"She got a bun in the oven. That's why she keeps paging me. Got caught up with some slick-ass New Orleans nigga and now I'm fitna be a grandfather."

"Why you ain't down there with her?"

He nodded toward the duplex up front, "Auntie needs me."

"Why she shake like that?"

"Parkinson's."

On screen, Church wore tight-ass shorts, a pair of high-top Adidas sneakers, an afro, and pork-chop sideburns. He shot the passing lane, stole the rock, then scored a layup on Darryl Dawkins. On the sofa, he pulled on the blunt, released a cloud of smoke, then inclined his head toward the television. "We need to get you up there."

I nodded without paying attention. *Church is somebody's Pops.* That fact had me shook.

"Young blood!"

"Say what?"

"I want to tape practice this week," he said. "It'll be good for you to see yourself in action, help you work through that hitch in your release."

Two weeks. That's how long I had to get my shit together. That, or get on a bus back to Kansas City and deal with Pops's shit.

Saturday rolled back around. I filled another grocery order for Ms. Rita. She let me in, cigarette steady dangling from the corner of her mouth. I put away her groceries and she made me coffee. I tried to decline, but it was hard to turn down an old woman who shook like that. She prepared mine with milk and sugar, but I could still taste a bitter, frozen flavor. We watched a *Jeopardy!* marathon. I left after the second episode. That night, she lost her balance in the bathroom, fell, and broke a hip. Church told me all about it before practice on Monday. I was standing at the line, shooting free throws.

"She had surgery yesterday," he said. "Doctors said she'll be home in a few days."

Church operated a camcorder from the sideline while I practiced. I shot jumpers and set shots from the top of the key, wings, corners; middies from both elbows; and little teardrop buckets around the rim. I was a little nervous, at first, but I soon forgot about the camera and focused on spreading my fingers, tucking in my elbow, snapping my wrist. Later, we played one-on-one and, to my surprise, I only lost by seven points.

"Better," Church said, tossing me a plastic grocery bag with something soft inside. I untied the handles and pulled out his green-and-white practice jersey from his days with the Sonics. It was reversible with his name and number, 8, on both sides.

"Yo!"

"Wore it my rookie year."

I held it up against my chest, imagined an announcer introducing me to a crowd of people at McNichols Arena. Then a sense of dread swelled up inside me. "You should keep this."

"You earned it." He offered me his hand. I took it and he pulled me in toward him for a one-handed hug, right shoulder to right shoulder. I froze. I'd come to understand what physical contact with Church meant on the court, him showing me how to pivot on the block, or him backing me down in the paint. But this?

"See that right there? The way you tensed up?" he whispered. "A teammate did that to me once. I retired at the end of the season. Because that's all it takes: the wrong person saying the wrong thing at the wrong time."

My face flashed hot with embarrassment. I fixed my lips to apologize, to condemn my stupidity, explain that I understood, but before I could say a word, Church clapped me on the shoulder then walked out of the gym.

"Ever have one of those moments you wish you could walk back?" I lean forward in a folding chair set above the free-throw line. Raquel sits across from me, and Neil stands behind the camera. The lamp blazes down on me, but doesn't bother me because, with just the three of us, the gym is a wide-open, drafty space.

"Why do you think you freaked out?" Raquel asks.

"Because I'm an asshole." It's one of few things about myself I know to be true.

"You were just a kid," Neil says.

"The worst kind."

"But, at this point," Raquel says, "you'd spent a few weeks working closely with Church—on and off the court. He never made a move on you, right?"

I shake my head.

"And you never had feelings like that for him?"

"No."

"So why did you panic?"

"I thought, maybe, he wanted something in return."

"For the jersey?" Neil pops his head out from behind the camera.

I nod.

"Do you still have it?" Raquel asks.

I stand and remove my sweatshirt, revealing Church's old practice jersey.

Neil adjusts the camera, zooming in, I suppose, on what remains of the flaky letters that spell *Seattle Supersonics*. I turn around so that Neil can get Church's name on the back.

"You thought he was bribing you for sex with that?" Disgust shades Neil's tone.

"You have to be a baller to understand," Raquel says. "My ex played point guard for Xavier. He sleeps in his practice jersey."

I pop mine away from my chest, "I wore this bad boy the very next day."

I skipped classes after lunch to visit Ms. Rita at Denver General. I brought flowers, partly to cheer her up, but also to make up for how I acted with Church the day before. I wore the jersey under a T-shirt because Church said we were still going to practice that afternoon. I couldn't wait to show it off at the King Center. All I had to do was visit Ms. Rita right quick, then dip. I wondered if Church was already at the hospital. *Maybe I can ride with him to the rec.* That thought slipped my mind the moment I walked into Ms. Rita's room.

Church stood on one side of her, a nurse stood on the other. Ms. Rita lay unmoving beneath folds of stiff, course blankets. Perspiration covered her head, which, free from her wig, was smooth with traces of fuzzy hair. My eyes fell on a tray of food: potatoes, carrots, and a piece of mystery meat covered in congealed gravy. The sharp odor of disinfectant overran my nostrils. It sat on my taste buds, acrid and unwelcome. I wanted then for Ms. Rita to sit up in bed and light one of her cigarettes, or for her to hand me a hot cup of instant coffee. I would breathe it in deeply, inhale its freeze dried-ness, try to ignore how pale and gaunt she had grown, almost as white as the linens that concealed her.

"Now's not a good time, young blood." Church's eyes shone sad and glassy.

A nurse swept into the room.

I set the flowers down by the cold hospital food. Church bent over, wiped her brow, whispered in her ear. I should not have been there, had no business witnessing their closeness. It felt wrong, illicit. The nurse's voice, when it made its way to my ears, carried words like *sepsis* and *fast moving* and *touch and go*. I followed her when she left, found a seat in reception. I sat there until it grew dark, until my stomach growled, until Church stumbled out, leaned against a wall, and slid down to the ground, face in hands.

Aljarita Denton, from Spencer, Oklahoma, was laid to rest one week before tryouts. Her service was held at a small Baptist church east of Colorado Boulevard. She was not a God-fearing woman, but the preacher eulogized her like she was the head of the women's auxiliary board. Others reminisced on her love of fried catfish, whiskey, and Alex Trebek, her ability to dispense kindness out one side of her mouth and curses out the other, and a disbelief that she'd died from sepsis.

"I always thought the cigarettes would get her," Church said, drawing a round of laughter. He explained how Ms. Rita, a single woman with no children, looked after him when he left home in the eighth grade; how she critiqued his performance on the court after each game she watched from the stands or, later, from her living room; how she required him to pay her half his earnings from a regular summer job with the postal service she arranged for him through an acquaintance; and how, when she visited him in Seattle, she admired his Bellevue home but worried about the vastness of his white neighbors.

You just a dash of pepper in a pot of rice!

"She was my family," Church said.

We watched tape after the funeral. Church smoked weed. I pretended to study the form of my three-point shot while keeping tabs on him out the corner of my eye. Each time he toked, the tip of the joint burned bright before cooling to ash. It conjured in my head old Sunday school lessons about man being made from ash and returning to ash. I tried to imagine Ms. Rita as a tiny heap, but each time I closed my eyes, I saw her sleeping face, pale and gaunt, in that hospital bed and this image was somehow worse.

Church rubbed at his eyes with the heel of his smoking hand. "Look at me," he said. "Acting like a little bitch." He said Ms. Rita would not have wanted his tears. The feeling of being an intruder struck me once more.

Someone knocked at the door.

Church answered it, joint still pinched between his fingers.

In stepped old boy I'd seen Church kissing five weeks earlier. That day seemed so long ago now, but I had no doubt it was him. Same crooked teeth. Same ratty beard. Same ill-fitting clothes. The brother averted his eyes when he saw me sitting there, started singing some sad song to Church. *Let me hold a little something 'til the first of the month.* Woot-di-woot-di-woot.

"Can't do it," Church said, nodding toward the door.

"You want me leaving here empty-handed, knowing what I know?"

Church hit him with that air-and-opportunity look.

"Aight," he said, opening the door to leave. "Bet."

"You ain't worried?" I asked Church.

"Life's too short, young blood." Church pulled on the joint, held in the smoke, and released that sticky aroma into the room. "Here," he said, nodding at the TV. "You squaring up with the basket, but you need to stop fading away. Jump straight up and hit them with that quick release."

It didn't take long for Church's business to get out in them streets. Now, whenever he left the gym, brothers mimicked a woman's switch and bent their wrists. At school, Tyree started asking me questions. *Why you walk like that? You the top or the bottom? He make you wash his drawls?* Junior put his two cents in one night after work.

"Yo, I didn't know he was that way," he said.

"What way?"

"You know what I mean."

"Why does it matter?"

Junior tried to make himself less round by straightening his back and spreading his shoulders apart. "He try something with you?" He looked around the store. "You *that way*, too?"

At least he asked. Gigi just stopped returning my calls. It's called ghosting nowadays. Back then, we called it getting kicked to the curb. Conjures up different images, but the feeling, like someone river dancing on your heart, hurts the same. I hated that pain, so I called until I got her on the phone.

"Why you ain't call me back?"

"Why you ain't tell me you gay?"

"I'm not," I said, reminding her of Labor Day and the front seat of her Honda.

The sound of sucking teeth came across the line. "Then why you spend so much time with that nigga? Why you let him talk to me like that? And why haven't we had sex yet?"

I was just about tell her why, but she started talking again.

"You know what, Davyon? Whatever. You wanna be gay? Be gay. But we can't kick it no more. It's a sin." She disconnected the call. I called back, but the phone rang until the answering machine came on. I was leaving a message when Mike picked up the line.

"Fall back little nigga!" I heard Dr. Hawkins protest in the background. *What did I tell you about answering my phone?* Mike ignored her. "Call here again and see if I don't come down to Junior's and kick your bitch ass up and down Dahlia Street!"

I didn't have words then for how I felt when I hung up the phone. It was anger, only more intense, like I might squab with the next dude I met named Mike. Jackson, Jordon, Tyson. Didn't matter. I just wanted to hit someone, anyone, named Mike, to feel the crack of bones, to watch blood gush from his nose, to keep on hitting him until my fists throbbed and I was tired of swinging.

Church swelled with disinterest. If having his name in everybody's mouth bothered him, he never said anything to me. Not on Monday and Tuesday, when he made me run suicides until I damn near passed out. Not on Wednesday, when he only beat me by five points in one-on-one. And not on Thursday, when Tyree and his crew swaggered into the gym in their Jackson High practice jerseys. Suddenly, brothers on the sideline waiting to play next—I'm talking about cats who done picked out a team!—start making room for Tyree and his boys. This is how they ended up playing in the very next game, running the defending team off the court like it was a warm-up drill. They were still playing two games later, when Bootleg Cheryl and I finally got on the court.

I stood in front of Tyree.

"Mismatch," Tyree called out.

I scanned the sideline. Church stood behind his camcorder next to the scoreboard. He nodded, and I nodded back.

"I knew y'all was butt buddies," Tyree said, checking up the ball.

I bounced it back and assumed a defensive stance.

He inbounded the ball then ran me off a screen that knocked me on my ass. He cut to the basket, where one of his guys fed him a bounce pass for an easy layup.

"Call out the goddamn screens!" I said, jumping up off the floor.

I raced down court to get in position for a jumper, but they trapped Bootleg Cheryl, so I ran back toward her.

She coughed up the rock, and the other team scored another quick bucket.

I ran point after that. They tried to trap me, but I split the defense and got across half court. I drove left on Tyree, dished the rock off to Bootleg, who shook her man with a head fake before pivoting toward the basket and banking the ball in off the glass.

"Who got Dorothy?" someone from the other team called out.

I was already down the other end of the court, telling my team to play defense. I picked-up Tyree at the top of the key and forced him left. He waved his team out of the lane so he could play me one-on-one. I watched his stomach, kept my knees bent and slid my feet so that I could stay in front of him. He backed me down into the paint. I braced him with the back of my forearm. It slowed him down but ain't stop him from shooting over me for another bucket.

"Nothing you can do about that," Church shouted.

I called for the rock, set-up one of my guys for a three-point bucket, but he bricked. Tyree rebounded the ball and dribbled toward our basket. He favored his right hand, so when one of my guys forced him left, I slid in front of him, made him pick up his dribble. Tyree held the ball over his head. Bootleg popped it out of his hands. I picked it up and raced down court. Footsteps trailed behind me. I took my steps, planted my left foot, and pushed myself away from the ground as hard as possible, reaching for the bucket with both hands.

Oooo, weee!

Yo, y'all see that?

Dorothy just dunked on Tyree!

My heart liked to jump out my chest, I was so hype. I played it cool, though, jogged back down court like ain't no thing but a chicken wing. Church played it cool, too, but it was something about his face that said he was happy. Not a smile but not a scowl, either. He hollered for me to d-up and it was gone. We lost the game, but not by much. Tyree and his crew left the gym. One of them came over to me on the low and dapped me up. "I see you, boy."

Saturday morning brought more old folks from Zion Senior Center. Mr. Hyde eyed me closely while I sliced up his order of hogshead cheese. It weighed in at just under a pound. He stared at the scale like he didn't believe it then nodded grudgingly. Later, I rounded up groceries for Church. I was packing everything into paper bags when Junior ambled over to the counter and told me that Church was no longer one of our customers.

"What happened?"

"Nothing happened." He wiped sweat from his forehead. "We just agreed he'd be better off buying his groceries from Safeway or King Soopers."

"But he's our best customer."

"My store, my rules."

It felt odd not seeing Church on a Saturday. Tryouts were two days away and I was bugging. I tried to distract myself with work. I organized shelves, cleaned windows, sanitized the slicer and grinder, and swept and mopped the floor.

Later that night, while Junior slept, I rewatched Church's NBA debut against Utah. He was nervous in that one. I watched him closely, tried to figure out how he conquered his jitters. The best I could make out is that he started playing better when he slowed down, let the game come to him. I wished I could be inside his head, wished I could know what he said to himself. Did he call himself a pussy, the way he'd done me that day? Or did he talk himself through each play? *You got this, Elijah. Just dribble. Split the defense. Open man. Drive. Dish.*

Monday. First day of tryouts. Nerves had me percolating, so I was glad when lunch came. It was still a grip of things to do between then and after school—a final exam on *The Clan of the Cave Bear* in World History and quadratic equations in Algebra—but at least I could go for a walk, burn off some nervous energy. I cut across the atrium. Tyree leaned against a wall with his crew. He muttered something and his homeboys laughed, but it was weak, like they ain't really mean it. This must have made him mad. Next thing I know, he following me down the hallway, calling me out my name: *punk, homo, limp-wristed ass bandit.* Woot-di-woot-di-woot. His boys tried to calm him down, but Tyree just stepped in front of me, blocking my path and steady talking out the side of his neck.

"And that nigga Church is a fucking fa—"

It hurt when my knuckles connected with Tyree's mouth. I cursed and shook my hand up and down, tried to get ready for my next blow, but shit got ill with a quickness. Hands holding me back. Arms throwing me into lockers. Me struggling to stay on my feet then falling to the ground, curling into a tight ball against an avalanche of fists and feet. It was like being back in Kansas City with Pops, but it was six of them and one of me.

Later, I sat in Dr. Hawkins's office with a bag of ice pressed to the side of my face. Junior sat next to me, mouth set in a tight line. Dr. Hawkins explained to him that she had no choice but to suspend me.

"What about the other guy?" Junior asked.

"Davyon threw the first punch, so he's the one who has to stay home for three days."

Junior sighed, but it sounded like a wheeze. "And tryouts?"

Dr. Hawkins stared at me over the rim of thick designer glasses then returned her attention to Junior. "Davyon is not to set foot on school property until Friday morning. Coach Mountainside is likely to have finalized his roster by then."

I opened my mouth to protest but Junior cut me off with a wave of his hand. "That seems extreme for a young man who was being picked on."

"I don't make the rules, Mr. Michaels." She sat back in her chair, elbows set on its arms, fingers folded together.

I flexed my fist, focused on the pain in my knuckles. The skin had already begun to tighten over them. Across the office suite, Tyree and Coach Mountainside shook hands with the principal, dipped out of his office, then slipped into the main hallway, disappearing amid a crush of students and security guards.

I wanted to go to the King Center that afternoon. Never mind how my lower lip throbbed, or how my eye was starting to bruise, or how the knuckles on my right hand were now swollen and tender. I needed to be on a court, to hold a ball, to feel that way I did each time I swished it through a net, that at least for a second—less than a second, a millisecond, or whatever's shorter than that—my life made sense.

"Rest today," Junior said. "We'll talk about everything else tomorrow."

Everything else.

Withdrawing from Jackson High at the end of the semester. Saving money for a bus ticket. That long ride back across the prairie to Kansas City. Home. Moms. Pops. And Church. *Everything else* also meant Church. Junior didn't want me around him anymore.

I swallowed some Tylenol then fished a bag of peas from the frozen food section and held it to my face for ten minutes at a time. Junior made me soak my knuckles in ice water. All that cold mixed with the air conditioner drove me outside. The sun was still hot for October. I stood there in its warmth, just beyond the shade of the awning, making and unmaking my fist. I didn't even notice the Jeep pull up until I heard the horn.

Church sat in the driver's seat. One look at his face told me he knew.

"Get in," he said.

I looked over my shoulder.

"Study long, study wrong."

At Jackson High, Church marched me right into the gym, which was four times the size of the King Center's. Five-on-five scrimmages were being played on multiple courts. It was a grip of brothers standing around the side-lines waiting for a chance to prove themselves. I tried to sit down on the bleachers, but Church pushed me ahead of him, marched me right into the middle of play, stop-ping the screech of sneakers and bouncing balls and brothers calling for the rock. A red ram, its horns bent back into tight coils, lay emblazoned on the hardwood at center court. I stood there beside Church. He demanded that Coach Mountainside let me lace up for tryouts. I started to protest but stopped because it would have been a lie. My sneakers were at home, but I'd run suicides bare-foot if it meant I might make the team.

Mountainside stood just as tall as Church but wider, like a tight end. He told Church that he could not let me try out.

Church pointed up to the wall where a 1968 championship banner hung.

"You know that's me, right?"

"I know everything I need to know about you," Mountainside said.

Church got that air-and-opportunity look again, but it was different somehow. The lines in his brow deepened more and it was something in his eyes, a decision maybe, before they narrowed to slits. He stepped toward Mountainside, who did not move. I pulled at the sleeve of Church's jacket, but he just shook me off.

"I'm the x-factor, nigga," he said to Mountainside. "You know what that means?"

Mountainside opened his mouth to speak.

"Means you don't know shit about me." He got up in the coach's face. "Not one god-damn thing." Then Church strode off the court like he just sank a winning bucket, and it was champagne waiting for him in the locker room. I struggled to match his stride.

"You see that?" he asked.

"See what?"

"How I ain't hit nobody."

The clock on the wall now reads one o'clock and the afternoon warmth has chased the chill from the gym at the King Center. Raquel stares at me, brow furrowed, mouth slack.

"That's it?" Neil asks. "You didn't tryout for the team?"

I shake my head. "Wasn't in the cards."

"But you worked so hard," Raquel says. "And, listen, that tape? Baybee! You gave Tyree Duncan the business—and he played at Seton Hall."

"He rode a bench at Seton Hall," I say.

"What happened when you went back to school?"

Tyree didn't mess with me after our fight. Junior said it was because I fought back. *Bullies don't like it when you do that.* Church had a different theory. *Bitch-ass nigga.* What I hadn't told either of them was that one of the homies, a shot caller, approached me when I returned to school after my suspension. His homeboys swaggered around me in a loose circle. *You got squabbles, homie.* He said I wouldn't have to worry about Tyree anymore, then held out a hundred-dollar bill. I took his money because I got the feeling that not taking it might have meant another ass whooping. Or worse. I thanked him, tried to stay on his good side with daps and nods when I saw him slanging on the block. I blew trees with him once. I should have been in P.E., but it was the last class of the day and, since I vowed never to set foot in the gym where I'd not been allowed to play, I always skipped it. Junior told me I would fail, but I didn't care. I'd just take P.E. again next semester. I'd be back at my high school in Kansas City by then. I'd already made plans with my old coach to practice with the team after winter break.

Junior and I still ate dinner in front of the television, watching old games. I didn't mind now that Church had shown me how to watch tape with a critical eye. One night, we rewatched a matchup between the Lakers and the Jazz in 1984. Kareem passing Wilt's all-time scoring record was Junior's favorite hoops moment. On first watch, I focused on Kareem swishing that skyhook from the right side of the baseline. Next time around, I noted that Kareem wouldn't have made that shot if Magic Johnson hadn't reset the offense to give Kareem time to post up Mark Eaton.

"So you an analyst now?" Junior grinned.

I was making money, too. Junior paid me wages once my suspension was over. I was free to spend it however I wanted, so long as I socked away enough money to cover my personal expenses and a bus ticket back to Kansas City. I worked every evening after school and most weekends. One Saturday, I peeped Mr. Hyde in front of the hogshead cheese, steady counting food stamps. I sliced up a pound, wrapped it, and priced it at fifty cents.

"Say now," he said, holding the package down and away from his face, studying the price through the bottom of his glasses. "That's all right."

Gigi and a couple of her girlfriends came into the store the day before Halloween. They pushed a cart up and down the aisles, occasionally busting into fits of laughter. They filled the counter with bags of candy, frozen pizzas, chips, soda, and a box of hohos. Gigi looked the same, only better. A glow radiated from her, like in cartoon fairytales. Her girlfriends flanked her, reminding me suddenly of Tyree's entourage.

"Hi," she said.

I nodded.

She gave one of her girls the keys to her car and told them she'd meet them outside.

One of them, South Africa, the one who tried to make me feel bad for drinking a Coke on Labor Day, shot me a dirty look on the way to the door.

"So," Gigi said when they were gone, "where do we go from here?"

I looked her dead in her eye without blinking.

She looked away, dug in her purse, then handed me some money. "Mama's not dating Mike anymore. She feels bad about the way he spoke to you."

"And how do you feel?"

She shrugged then invited me to Celebrities that weekend.

I made change, wrote a message on the back of her receipt, handed it to her.

She smiled then read the message. "Kick rocks? Really?"

I nodded toward the bags. "Need help with that?"

Her smiled faded. She collected her bags, then walked off in a huff. She still comes in the store from time to time, but we never speak. She's First Lady now at a mega church in Aurora.

I bought a pair of Air Revolutions with my first check. The Jackson High players rocked black ones with red and gray trim. I copped the white joints with red and navy accents. They felt like butter on my feet when I hooped at the King Center. Twenty-one, one-on-one, five-on-five: I played anything. Just no drills. I wanted to flex my new game, not train to death. Plus, it was easy to get on the court now. All I had to do was walk in the gym, and somebody would call out to me. *Yo, Davyon, wanna run?* That's how it happened one day, and my team ran everybody out the gym.

Church and I played one-on-one that November. Outside, there was snow on the ground. Inside, the front desk was decked-out with little cardboard turkey and pilgrim cutouts. He had just sold the duplex on Holly Street. In just a few days, he would be settling into a home in New Orleans near Celeste, now in her eighth month of pregnancy. He was waiting for me when I walked into the rec that afternoon. We traded buckets in a friendly game of one-on-one. I played strong, confident even. Still, Church only let me get so close, ending the game on a fade-away jumper from downtown.

"And that was the last time you saw him?" Raquel asks.

I nod. "I went back to Kansas City." I don't explain how Pops and I struck an uneasy truce that lasted the better part of a year before life in our household returned to business as usual—only worse. Pops, having restrained himself all those months, leaned into his cruelty. I was a senior in high school the next time we fought. Santana, home on leave from the marines, and not yet out to the family, had to pull me off him. I am grateful he'd been there that day. I might have killed him otherwise. Then what? Prison? Probation? A life of checking that box on job applications? No. This time, I put myself on a bus to Denver. Went back to Junior, worked for him full time while I got my GED, then attended Metro State part-time. It took me a grip to earn a business degree, but that's where I met Xiomara, fell in love, lived something close to a life.

"Ever play anywhere?" Raquel asks.

Neil is aghast when I say *no*, but Raquel seems to get it, though I am not sure what, exactly, *it* is. That basketball is just a game? That hoop dreams are just that—dreams? Or maybe it has something to do with the scarcity of imagination, our failure to grasp the abundance of what could be, that our lives are big enough to hold more than one dream? Raquel talks about Church, how for as long as she can remember, he'd been there for her and her mother, Celeste. Taught her to swim and ride a bike. Coached her middle school and high school hoop squads. Paid for film school. It is hard to listen to her reminisce on Church. Her inner life is lush and verdant, watered by love and belonging. Mine is as brittle as the letters peeling away on the jersey Church gave me.

Raquel promises to send me a draft of the documentary for *peer-review* before releasing it, a revelation that lessens the weight I've felt throughout the interview. I leave the King Center feeling lighter than I have since Pops announced he was coming to town. With any luck, by this time tomorrow, he'll be halfway back to Kansas City. I roll down the windows in my car, let the brisk autumn air rush over me all the way back to the Dahlia, where I find Pops's truck parked outside the store. Something inside me drops. I park, jump out, and stride over to the pickup, determined to have it out with him, but the cab is empty. I march toward the store, my hands clenched into fists. If last night is any indication, if what I'd seen on camera was right, then Pops is drinking again. I won't have him making a scene in my store.

Xiomara meets me at the door, ushers me off to the side away from customers.

"He's in the café," she says, nodding to a corner of the store where customers, mostly senior citizens, sit, their hands filled with books, devices, crochet needles. There, in their midst, sits Pops nursing a can of something while writing in a book. He's smaller than the last time I'd seen him, and without a hat, the gray of his hair is more noticeable. It's a good move on his part, pinning me down in public, my place of business, no less, where I am less likely to tell an old man to go fuck himself, which I realize right then is not really what I want to do. I am not sure what I want to say, but standing there next to Xiomara, who still believes in me, tapers my anger.

"He drunk?"

"Sober as a judge when he walked in a two hours ago."

"What's in the can?"

"Kombucha," she says. "From our deli."

I think about the cans I saw on camera the night before and it all makes sense. The only thing worse than the taste of beer is Kombucha, so it tracks that Pops likes it.

"And the book?" I ask.

"Sudoku," she says. "Wanna take the rest of the day off?"

There's an idea. Pops likely hasn't clocked me yet. I can play hooky, spend the rest of the day in a bookstore, or at the movies getting lost in the problems of imaginary people while munching on popcorn, or treat myself to an early dinner—something not on a deli menu. A big steak, seafood, or a plate of spaghetti and meatballs. Thoughts of food, though, conjure up my promise to Moms, that I'd think about coming home for Thanksgiving, and that brings me back around to the man solving puzzles and sipping a fermented beverage in my store. It makes sense that Church's voice fills my head in that moment. *Air and opportunity, young blood. Air and opportunity.* Damned if I know what kind, but I won't find out hiding by the restrooms with Xiomara. I squeeze her shoulder, walk over to Pops's table, and sit my ass down.

VINCE OMNI is author of *1989*, winner of the CRAFT 2025 Novelette Print Prize. Other awards include a PEN/Dau Short Story Prize, the Jesmyn Ward Prize in Fiction, and the Margaret Walker Memorial Prize in Creative Writing. His writing has appeared in the *Michigan Quarterly Review*, *The Best Debut Short Stories 2025,* and is forthcoming in *Virgin Islands Noir*. Vince holds an MFA from the University of Kansas and a PhD from Florida State University, where he was a McKnight Doctoral Fellow. He teaches African American literature and creative writing at Lake Forest College and is cofounder of *SoulClap: A Black Joy Journal.*

www.ingramcontent.com/pod-product-compliance
Lightning Source LLC
Chambersburg PA
CBHW060339310726
48976CB00007B/2619